OCEANS

Greg Roza

Rosen Classroom Books & Materials™
New York

Published in 2006 by The Rosen Publishing Group, Inc.
29 East 21st Street, New York, NY 10010

Copyright © 2006 by The Rosen Publishing Group, Inc.

All rights reserved. No part of this book may be reproduced in any form without permission in writing from the publisher, except by a reviewer.

Book Design: Jennifer Crilly

Photo Credits: Cover, p. 1 © Jason Childs/Getty Images; p. 5 © 2002 GeoAtlas; p. 6 © Stephen Studd/Getty Images; p. 9 © OAR/National Undersea Research Program (NURP), NOAA; p. 10 © Ed Simpson/Getty Images; p. 13 © Endeavor-NASA/Getty Images; p. 14 © Wolcott Henry/National Geographic/Getty Images; p. 17 © Steven Hunt/Getty Images; p. 18 © David Fleetham/Getty Images; p. 20 © Darlyne A. Murawski/National Geographic/Getty Images

ISBN: 1-4042-5825-6
6-pack ISBN: 1-4042-5826-4

Manufactured in the United States of America

Contents

Earth's Oceans	4
Oceans and the Water Cycle	7
Saltwater	8
Oceans and Earth's Weather	11
The Ocean Floor	12
Ocean Creatures	15
Sunlit Zone	16
Twilight Zone	19
Midnight Zone	21
Adapting to Life in the Ocean	22
Glossary	23
Index	24

Earth's Oceans

Oceans cover almost three-quarters of Earth's surface and hold about ninety-seven percent of Earth's water. There are five oceans: the Atlantic, Pacific, Indian, Arctic, and Antarctic. The Pacific Ocean covers almost one-third of Earth's surface!

Earth's oceans are all connected by smaller bodies of water, such as seas and gulfs. Most of Earth's living things live in the oceans. The oceans are home to everything from tiny plants to the giant blue whale.

Oceans cover about seventy percent of Earth's surface.

Oceans and the Water Cycle

Oceans play the biggest part in the **water cycle**. The sun's heat turns some of the water in the oceans to **water vapor**. Water vapor rises into the air and forms clouds. Water vapor then cools and falls back to Earth as rain or snow. When it hits the ground, much of it forms streams and rivers, which eventually flow back to the ocean. Then the cycle starts over again.

Ocean water supplies almost all of the moisture that makes rain. Life on Earth couldn't exist without rainfall.

Saltwater

Water found in the oceans and seas is called saltwater. Saltwater makes up ninety-seven percent of Earth's water. Much of the salt in Earth's oceans comes from the **erosion** of rocks on land. Rivers break down rocks and **minerals**, which include salts, and carry them to the oceans. Less than three percent of Earth's water is freshwater. We use freshwater for drinking, bathing, and watering our crops.

Some of the ocean's salt comes from cracks on the ocean floor called vents.

Oceans and Earth's Weather

The oceans help to warm the air when it is cold and cool the air when it is hot. In the summer, ocean water takes in heat from the sun and stores it. In the winter, the ocean can release stored heat to warm the air.

Ocean currents affect Earth's weather patterns. Currents are caused by warm water rising to the surface and cold water sinking below the surface. They are also caused by the movement of wind on the ocean's surface.

The oceans are the main source of the rainwater that falls to Earth, refilling rivers and lakes with freshwater.

The Ocean Floor

Like the land on the continents, the ocean floor has vast plains, tall mountains, volcanoes, and deep valleys. The deepest parts of the oceans are great cracks called **trenches**.

When you step into the ocean, you are standing on part of a continent called a continental shelf. At about 600 feet, the continental shelf drops off to a steeper area called the continental slope. This area drops down over two miles to the ocean basin. The ocean basin is mostly flat land.

Islands are actually the tops of tall mountains and volcanoes that have risen above the surface of the ocean.

Ocean Creatures

There is a wide variety of plants and animals in the ocean. Plankton are tiny plants and animals that do not move by themselves. They drift with the ocean currents.

The ocean has many animals that swim, such as fish, octopuses, and dolphins. Some ocean animals spend time on land, such as seals and turtles. Animals such as starfish, sponges, and coral have **adaptations** that enable them to cling to rocks, the ocean floor, and other animals.

The ocean floor is home to many sea creatures, such as coral and blue starfish.

Sunlit Zone

Scientists divide the ocean into different life zones. The top zone is the sunlit zone. This layer can reach down about 600 feet below the surface. It receives the most light from the sun. More than ninety percent of all the **open ocean's** creatures live in this zone. Sea plants need sunlight, so most of them live in this zone. Many animals of the sunlit zone feed on the plentiful plant life found there. This zone is home to many kinds of fish, **mammals**, and plankton.

Creatures such as sea turtles live in the sunlit zone where there is plenty of plant life to feed on.

Twilight Zone

The twilight zone lies between 600 and 3,000 feet beneath the surface. This layer is darker than the sunlit zone because less sunlight reaches it. Very few plants live in this zone because they cannot get enough light. Since there are fewer plants, there are also fewer animals. Fish living in the twilight zone eat other fish that live there. They may also swim up to the sunlit zone to feed. Twilight zone animals include some jellyfish, lantern fish, and sharks.

Some of the twilight zone's animals have adaptations to help them live in the darkness. Some jellyfish can produce their own light.

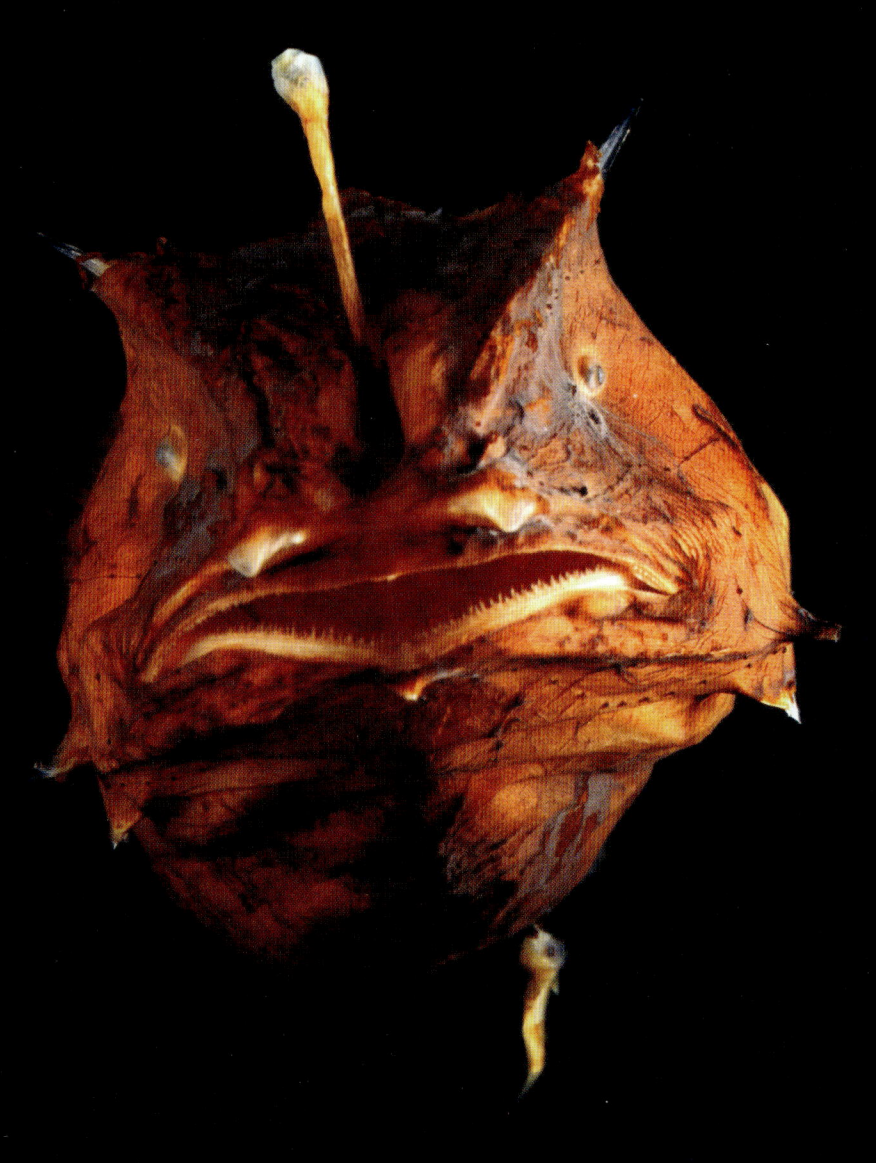

Midnight Zone

The midnight zone makes up about ninety percent of the ocean. No sunlight reaches the midnight zone. The water **pressure** is very heavy, and the water **temperature** is often very cold. Very few creatures can live there. The midnight zone reaches down to the ocean floor, which has cracks called vents. These vents release boiling water from deep within Earth's crust. Tiny creatures live around these vents. Other deep-sea animals—such as eel and tube worms—feed on these tiny creatures.

Some types of angler fish are able to live in the cold, dark depths of the midnight zone.

Adapting to Life in the Ocean

Over millions of years, creatures have developed adaptations for living in their surroundings. Some mammals, such as the elephant seal, can hunt for food underwater for twenty minutes before returning to the surface for air. The animals that live in the twilight and midnight zones can withstand great pressure and cold temperatures. Some fish that live in these zones are able to make their own light! These adaptations allow creatures to live in Earth's oceans.

Glossary

adaptations   Traits that allow living things to live and survive in their environment.

erosion   The wearing away of land over time.

mammals   Animals that have backbones and feed their babies milk from their bodies.

minerals   Something found in nature that is not an animal or plant.

open ocean   The area of the ocean away from coastal waters.

pressure   A force that pushes on something.

temperature   How hot or cold something is.

trenches   Deep cracks on the floor of the ocean.

water cycle   The process by which water evaporates from plants, animals, and bodies of water, and returns as rain and snow.

water vapor   Tiny drops of water in the air.

Index

A
adaptations, 15, 22

C
continental shelf, 12
continental slope, 12
currents, 11, 15

E
erosion, 8

F
freshwater, 8

M
mammals, 16, 22
midnight zone, 21–22
minerals, 8

O
ocean floor, 12, 15, 21
open ocean, 16

P
plankton, 15–16
pressure, 21–22

S
saltwater, 8
sunlit zone, 16, 19
surface, 4, 11, 16, 19, 22

T
temperature, 21–22
trenches, 12
twilight zone, 19, 22

W
water cycle, 7
water vapor, 7
weather, 11